Aladdin

STERLING CHILDREN'S BOOKS
New York

A STORY FROM
Arabian Nights

ILLUSTRATIONS BY
Francesca Rossi

TEXT ADAPTATION GIADA FRANCIA

GRAPHIC DESIGN MARINELLA DEBERNARDI

Long ago in a distant city in Arabia, there lived a woman. She had been a widow for a long time, and had a son named Aladdin. She was a dressmaker, but the work brought in barely enough to take care of them.

Aladdin was a rebellious young man. He was stubborn and sometimes disobedient. As soon as he was old enough to learn a trade, his mother took him to her workshop. She began to show him how to work with the needle. But no matter how she tried, it was impossible to teach him. As soon as her back was turned, Aladdin would run off to wander through the narrow streets of the city. Sometimes he did not return home until evening. He often passed entire days like this, without a care in the world and with no real interest in anything. His only companion was his pet monkey, who followed him everywhere.

One day, while wandering aimlessly in the bazaar, he collided with a stranger and accidentally pushed him to the ground. Aladdin apologized and helped the man up.

When the stranger looked up, anger disappeared from his face and gave way to a smug grin. This mysterious person was, in fact, a sorcerer. He had arrived in the city two days earlier with the sole purpose of finding Aladdin.

The sorcerer had spent years looking for him. He didn't know his name or where he lived, but his face had appeared again and again in his crystal ball. All he knew was that Aladdin was the only one who could help him carry out his plan.

"Are you hurt?" asked Aladdin.

"Not at all," replied the sorcerer. Then he added a lie, hoping to win Aladdin's trust: "You are so thoughtful! You remind me of your father when he was young. You look so much like him, too!"

"You knew my father?" Aladdin asked, astonished.

"Of course," lied the sorcerer. "I was one of his dearest friends! Come on, I'll buy you lunch, and we can talk."

The sorcerer led Aladdin into a nearby tavern.

"Aladdin, I'm so glad to have met you," the sorcerer said a few hours later. "I have been traveling for many years. I didn't think I would get to know the son of my old friend when I returned home! Now that I've met you I feel closer to your father. I hope you will think of me as a dear uncle."

"Yes, I . . . gladly," replied Aladdin, who was feeling a little uncomfortable. He had never been in such a stylish tavern and had never eaten such good food! He was lucky

to have met this old friend of his father. *Who knows how he has become so rich?* he thought.

Almost guessing his thoughts, the sorcerer said, "I imagine that you, Aladdin, have taken up your father's work."

"No. That is, not right now . . ."

"But, my dear boy, you cannot spend every day hanging around!"

"Yes, I know. I've often been told that."

"Well, I can teach you how to become as rich as me, if you like."

"Yes!" Aladdin replied enthusiastically. "Sure! I would love to."

"Well, let's not waste any more time then. First of all, you must come with me to the Mountain of Spirits."

"What? But it's beyond the desert! Why do we have to go down there?" Aladdin asked, surprised.

"Trust me. You will become richer than you ever imagined. We leave tomorrow, at dawn."

Aladdin was convinced, and decided to embark on the mysterious journey.

The following day they set off, the sorcerer riding his camel while Aladdin walked by their side. The sorcerer told many amusing stories to brighten the journey and make the fatigue more bearable. After many hours, the Mountain of Spirits appeared on the horizon. Finally, they arrived at the foot of a mountain and entered a very narrow valley.

"Let's stop here," the sorcerer said.

He wanted to bring Aladdin to that fateful place because he needed him to help carry out his grand plan. He asked Aladdin to gather some dry twigs to light a fire. When Aladdin returned with a bundle of sticks, the sorcerer spoke to him:

"You are going
to witness many
wonders that no
one has seen before."

The sorcerer sat on the ground and took out his crystal ball.

"You're a magician!" cried Aladdin in astonishment.

"One of the most powerful," said the sorcerer, lighting the fire. "But my crystal ball reveals that you, my dear boy, are the only person able to enter the cave. And you'll do it for me."

"Me? What? But there's no cave here."

The magician pulled a bunch of herbs out of a bag, and threw it into the flames. The earth shook and burst open at their feet, revealing the entrance to a narrow cavern.

"At the far end of this cave lies a hidden treasure that will make you richer than the greatest sultan on Earth. You will see many amazing things in there, but you must only look for a lighted lamp. Take it, extinguish the flame, and bring it to me. Now go, my boy. And remember: soon we'll both be rich for life!"

With one effortless leap, Aladdin was underground. As he entered the cave, he was struck by an extraordinary spectacle.

Aladdin had stumbled upon a garden full of strange trees, which were laden with exquisite fruits. He looked closer and found that the colorful fruits were actually precious gems! The white fruits were pearls; the ones that were sparkling and transparent were diamonds; the pink and blue fruits were sapphires; and the green ones were emeralds. All were of a size and perfection never before seen anywhere in the world.

At the foot of the trees lay piles of gold. Aladdin seized handfuls of the treasure and filled his pockets. When he could no longer cram any more gold in, he plucked the gems from the trees and hid them inside his shirt. Then he removed his belt and stuffed gems into the folds of his pants.

"The magician was right," Aladdin said to himself gleefully. "We're going to be rich for life!"

Weighed down with so much wealth, he continued nonetheless through the cave. At the end of the garden, he came across a staircase. He climbed fifty steps and finally reached a terrace. There, he saw the soft glow of a single

flame. It was the lighted lamp that the old magician had described to him.

Remembering his instructions, Aladdin extinguished the flame and grabbed the lamp. Then he retraced his steps and returned to the cave entrance. The sorcerer was waiting impatiently.

"Please, give me your hand and help me up," said Aladdin.

"Give me the lamp first," the sorcerer demanded.

"I'll give it to you as soon as I'm out of here," replied Aladdin, who did not quite trust the magician. And he was right to be wary: the sorcerer had planned to take the lamp and leave Aladdin trapped in the cave forever! He had never intended to share the wealth.

Exasperated by the boy's refusal, the sorcerer was overcome with rage. If Aladdin wasn't going to give him the lamp, then he would have to get it himself! He decided to use a spell, and threw more herbs on the fire while uttering some magic words. But the spell backfired: as soon as he spoke the magic words, a great rock rolled across the cave entrance, sealing it.

Aladdin began to shout and beat his fists against the stone. When he realized that he could not move the rock, he tried to think of a way out of the terrible situation.

"Perhaps there is another entrance," he wondered aloud. "But how will I find it?"

The cave was now very dark. Suddenly he remembered the old lamp. He pulled it out of his pocket and rubbed it to light it.

A spiral of blue smoke began to rise out of the lamp—slowly at first, then faster and faster, until it filled every corner of the large cavern. Aladdin dropped the lamp, which began to spin on the ground. Then, by some invisible force, it rose into the air.

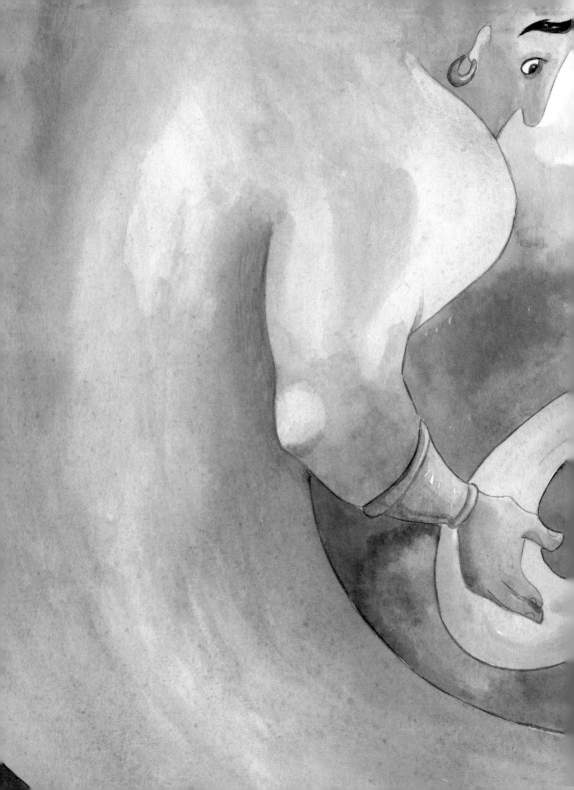

A sudden flash of blue light forced Aladdin to cover his face with his hands. When the young man finally lowered his hands, he was shocked by what appeared before him. It was a huge genie, hovering in midair.

"You have freed me!" cried the genie, bowing to Aladdin. "The lamp has been my prison for thousands of years. I am grateful, my master. Your wish is my command."

Aladdin was stunned. He thought he was dreaming, and so he said the first thing that came into his head: "Take me back home at once."

No sooner had he uttered these words, than the earth burst open. In an instant he was outside the cave, at the spot where the sorcerer had left him. The genie lifted him in his large arms. Together, they flew back along the route Aladdin had taken that morning. Soon Aladdin found himself at home, calling loudly for his mother. He wanted to show her the lamp and the precious stones he had collected in the cave.

"Our troubles are over!" he declared. "First, we will build a new shop for you, one that is bigger and brighter. You can stop doing small repairs and finally use your talents to make clothes for wealthy ladies. Isn't that what you have always wanted? What do you say?"

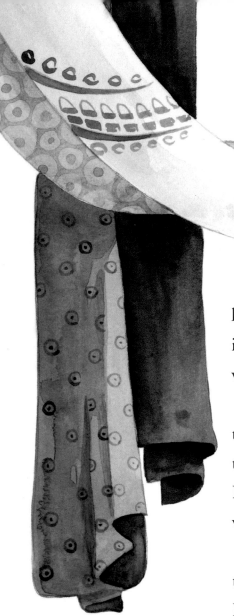

"It seems wonderful, Aladdin," said his mother, excited. "I can't believe it. But there is one thing I must ask: what will you do?"

Aladdin looked down at the lamp thoughtfully. He thought about all the trouble he had caused his mother. He thought about all the days he had wasted wandering through the city.

"It's strange," he said slowly. "Now that I'm rich, I could go anywhere I please. I could even spend all day in

bed if I wanted. But I feel the need for something more. With the help of the genie, I would like to become a cloth merchant. I can work with you in the new shop, and I won't go off wandering around the streets anymore."

He embraced his astonished mother.

"And now, Genie, how about organizing a banquet for me and my mother? We have plenty to celebrate."

Instantly, dinner was served. The genie appeared, carrying a large silver tray. The tray held twelve gold dishes of delicious food, two bottles of excellent wine, and two crystal cups. He put everything on the table and then disappeared.

From that day on, Aladdin took pleasure and pride in his work. He imported rare and precious fabrics from distant countries with the help of the genie. In a few short weeks, the young man became known as a reliable merchant, supplying the finest damask drapes and embroidered silks.

One morning, while Aladdin was working in the bazaar, the sultan's guards appeared and ordered everyone indoors. The princess had just returned to the city, and this was the route that they were taking to the palace. No one was allowed to see her.

The princess, however, did not wish to be hidden. She wanted to be among her people. But despite her wishes, the guards always kept her away from anyone who was not royalty. Most of her days were spent locked up inside the walls of the palace.

When they passed through the bazaar, the princess snuck away. She quickly ducked into a fortune teller's shop before the guards could stop her.

It was there that Aladdin glimpsed her. The young man was in the old fortune teller's shop when she entered. *How I would like to see her face,* he thought. And as if he had said the words aloud, his pet monkey took a great leap and landed on the princess's shoulder. The monkey lifted her veil for a moment, uncovering the princess's beautiful face. Aladdin was dazzled by her beauty and fell in love instantly.

That evening, at home with his mother, Aladdin could not help sighing all the way through dinner. She was surprised to see him sad and dreamy. It was so unlike him. She asked if something had happened, or perhaps he did not feel well. When her son started to explain, she listened very carefully. He finally confessed that he wanted to ask for the princess's hand in marriage.

At that point, she started to laugh. "Oh, my son! You must have lost your mind!"

But then, seeing that Aladdin was being serious, she decided to help him. She offered to take a gift to the sultan—the precious stones that the young man had found in the cave. In the light of the sun, the gems were breathtaking. Their variety of color, their splendor, and their luster dazzled both mother and son. Aladdin hoped that the sultan would be impressed by them and would agree to meet with him.

Aladdin's mother took the pot of precious stones and made her way to the sultan's palace. When she arrived, the guards took her into a beautiful room. She was very nervous, but tried to compose herself as she greeted the sultan and his advisers. Trembling, she offered the gift to the sultan and asked him to meet her son. Hearing the answer, she went home with a light heart.

"He will meet with you, Aladdin!" she said when she returned. "Your gift has intrigued him, and he wants to know what you have to say."

"When can I go to him? When can I ask for the princess's hand in marriage?"

"In exactly one month!"

"A month? That's too long! I can't wait that long," said Aladdin. He grabbed the lamp and summoned the genie.

"What is your desire?" the genie asked when he appeared.

Aladdin explained to him that he had to see the princess. He must talk to her, and show her that he loved her. The genie nodded. With a wave of his hand, he conjured up a magic carpet—a carpet that could fly up to the princess's window, which was at the top of the highest tower in the palace.

As soon as Aladdin sat on the carpet, it lifted off the ground and began circling the room. Then it flew out the window and took him up into the clouds. Aladdin soon discovered that he was able to guide the carpet with his thoughts. He directed it to the sultan's palace.

When he reached the palace, all the lights were off—except for one room at the top of a tower. The princess was still awake!

The princess had not been able to sleep. She was furious! During dinner, yet another suitor had been presented to her. He was one of the richest and most noble men in the land. But she had refused the suitor.

"You must make up your mind," the sultan had implored. "In three days it will be your birthday. Then, according to the law, you must marry."

Back in her room, the princess had started pacing back and forth. She only wanted to marry for love. And more than anything else, she wanted to get out of the palace! At that moment, she heard a noise outside the window. She leaned out and was astonished to see a young man sitting on a rug, floating in front of her window.

"Your Highness, I know this seems crazy, but if you would listen to me for a few minutes . . ."

"Take me away!"

"What?" Aladdin asked in amazement.

"Let me get on your carpet! Help me get out of the palace!"

The boy could not believe what he was hearing. He moved the carpet closer to the window and the princess climbed on. Together, they flew away.

And so began an unforgettable night for Aladdin and the princess. They flew over the city, talking for hours. The princess immediately fell in love with this young man who was so bold and different, and who had dared to help her escape.

Sunrise came all too soon, and the two young people returned to the palace. As they approached, they saw a crowd gathered in the courtyard. The princess's disappearance had been discovered and the sultan was ordering the guards to find her. When the carpet landed, the princess ran up to her father and introduced him to Aladdin.

"Your Magnificence," he said. "I love your daughter. Please permit me to marry her."

"How dare you!" the sultan replied angrily. "You are not worthy of my daughter!"

"Father, you said that I must marry before my birthday! I choose Aladdin."

The sultan knew only too well how stubborn she was. He would not be able to change her mind, so he thought of a way to avoid the marriage.

"I will allow you to marry her if you can build a palace in three days." Then he added:

"If you fail,
you will
die!"

The princess protested, but Aladdin smiled and raced home to the lamp.

"What is your command, young master?" said the genie, emerging from the lamp.

"You must help me win the princess's hand by building the largest palace the city has ever seen. You have three days."

"Three days?" laughed the genie. "I only need three hours. Watch!"

With sudden flashes of light, the genie started to throw up the walls of a grand palace.

After three hours, the genie had completed his task.

"My young master, your palace is finished," the genie said with a proud expression on his face. "Come! See if you like my work."

He transported the young man into the palace. Aladdin was breathless with wonder as he walked through the halls. The place was filled with elegant ornaments and magnificent decorations. It was truly worthy of the princess.

When the people of the city awoke the next morning, everyone was astounded to see Aladdin's beautiful palace. News of this incredible wonder spread very quickly. The sultan had no choice but to keep his promise.

The wedding of Aladdin and the princess was celebrated just a week later. It was a festival that lasted for days, and all the guests were delighted by the music and dancing at the wedding banquet. Even the sultan was so impressed that he had to confess he'd never seen anything like it in his own palace.

While the party was in full swing, the evil sorcerer who had shut Aladdin in the cave was gazing into his precious crystal ball. Up to that moment, he had been sure that Aladdin had perished miserably in the cavern. But he now decided to find out for sure what had become of him.

Looking into the crystal ball, he was shocked to discover that Aladdin had been rescued. Not only had he managed to escape the cave, but he was now living in great splendor! He was immensely rich. He had even become the honored and respected husband of a princess. The sorcerer was furious.

"That boy has discovered the secret of the lamp!" he hissed.

The next morning, he jumped into the saddle of his camel and set off. Very soon, he arrived at the sultan's city and devised a plan to steal the lamp. First, he had to find out where the lamp was, and see if Aladdin took it with him everywhere he went. He drew out the crystal ball and was pleased to find that Aladdin was out on a journey to buy new fabrics—the lamp had been left behind in his palace. The sorcerer had to act at once!

The magician went to the bazaar and bought new lamps. Then, posing as a dealer in rare objects, he went to the palace. After persuading the guards, he was permitted to meet with the princess.

As he sipped tea with the princess, the sorcerer saw the magic lamp standing on the table. It was exactly as he had seen it in the crystal ball.

"I'm surprised to see that a lady as elegant as Your Highness has such an old and shabby lamp in her home. I would be honored if you were to exchange it for one of mine. They are more beautiful and far more valuable!"

The princess had no idea that Aladdin's lamp was magical. She accepted a new lamp with pleasure.

As soon as the magician had the old lamp in his hands, he rubbed it. The genie appeared and bowed to his new master. The sorcerer cackled.

"Take me and the princess and this entire palace far away from here. And make sure Aladdin goes back to being the penniless good-for-nothing that he once was!"

The genie was furious. He tried to resist, but the magic that bound him to the lamp was too strong. The genie had to do as the sorcerer said.

When Aladdin returned from his trip and realized what had happened, he despaired.

"Where shall I find my princess?" he asked himself. "Where is my palace? And how can I find them without the genie's help?"

Aladdin was heartbroken. For days he would not speak. Neither his mother nor the sultan was able to cheer him up. Even his pet monkey tried to make him smile, but for the first time she failed.

"My little monkey, I can't stop thinking about the princess. I wish I could go back to the day I met her, to the moment I first saw her, when I was stuck in the fortune teller's shop, and . . . Wait!" he cried, jumping to his feet. "I have an idea! The fortune teller understands magic. If there is one person in the whole city who can help me find them, it is her!"

Aladdin raced to the fortune teller's shop, with the monkey clinging to his shoulder. He had not been there for a long time, and he almost missed the entrance. It was hidden behind a heavy tapestry embroidered with stars and moons.

"I've been waiting for you," the fortune teller said as Aladdin entered the shop. "It's been a long time since we last met. It was the day the princess came to me to know her future. I predicted that she would meet a brash young man and fall in love. And that one day she would disappear with the palace he had built for her. But she didn't believe me."

"You already know everything! You know what happened to her!"

"I know that a sorcerer has taken her away."

"How can I find them?"

"Magic always leaves a trail. I can follow it and show you the way."

As soon as the fortune teller had revealed the place where the magician had taken the princess, Aladdin ran to his mother's house. He still had the flying carpet, and the sorcerer did not know about it.

Aladdin flew faster than the wind. In a few short hours, he arrived in the middle of the desert where his palace now stood. The carpet dropped Aladdin right under the windows of the princess's room.

The little monkey climbed up onto the ledge, attracting the princess's attention. She was surprised to see Aladdin's pet. Then she leaned out the window and saw Aladdin himself. Happy and excited, she was about to call out his name when he motioned for her to be quiet.

"Is the sorcerer here?" he whispered.

"Yes, he's here! I have been so frightened, Aladdin. What do we do now?"

"I have a plan. Invite the sorcerer to join you for tea and keep him talking."

"No! I hate that man!"

"My dear, please do as I say! In the meantime, I will steal the lamp."

"I wish you had told me about the genie. It certainly would have saved us a lot of trouble," the princess said angrily.

"Yes, I was wrong. I promise I won't keep things from you anymore. But now, go!"

As soon as he saw the princess having tea with the sorcerer, Aladdin crept into the palace. He crossed the courtyard and climbed the stairs to the room where the sorcerer had kept the lamp. When he tried to open the door, however, he found it locked. There was a tiny window above the door, but Aladdin would never be able to fit through it.

"How am I going to get in?" he wondered aloud. Aladdin looked at his pet monkey and was struck with an idea. "It's up to you, my little friend. Go up there and get the lamp!"

The monkey leaped into the air and grasped onto the window ledge with her tail. She swung herself into the room and grabbed the lamp, quickly returning it to Aladdin. As soon as he had it in his hands, Aladdin summoned the genie.

"Hello, young master. I've missed you!" the genie said with a smile. "What is your command?"

"I would like you to take us home. And take the evil sorcerer someplace far away where he can never hurt us again!"

"Your wish is my command."

The palace and everything in it became surrounded in a cloud of blue smoke. When the smoke cleared, Aladdin and the princess found that the palace had been returned to its rightful place.

But the genie's work was not done. With a puff of breath, he created a whirlwind that captured the sorcerer and carried him to the other side of the world. The sorcerer found himself in a snowy valley surrounded by towering mountains, from which he would be unable to escape.

When the genie finally returned to Aladdin, the young man had a surprise for him.

"I have one last wish for you, my magic friend. I want to break the spell of the lamp. You are free to go wherever you want and do just as you wish."

The genie stared at Aladdin in disbelief. Then he began to laugh for joy. He rose into the air and flew to the stars, enjoying freedom for the first time in thousands of years.

STERLING CHILDREN'S BOOKS
New York

An Imprint of Sterling Publishing
387 Park Avenue South
New York, NY 10016

STERLING CHILDREN'S BOOKS and the distinctive Sterling Children's Books logo are registered
trademarks of Sterling Publishing Co., Inc.

First Sterling edition 2015
First published in Italy in 2014 by De Agostini Libri S.p.A.

ISBN 978-1-4549-1506-5

Distributed in Canada by Sterling Publishing
c/o Canadian Manda Group, 165 Dufferin Street
Toronto, Ontario, Canada M6K 3H6
For information about custom editions, special sales, and premium and corporate purchases,
please contact Sterling Special Sales at 800-805-5489 or specialsales@sterlingpublishing.com.

Translation: Contextus s.r.l., Pavia, Italy (Louise Bostock)
Editor: Contextus s.r.l., Pavia, Italy (Martin Maguire)

Manufactured in China
Lot #:
2 4 6 8 10 9 7 5 3 1
11/14
www.sterlingpublishing.com/kids